# Jakers!™

# Ferny Gets a Crush

adapted by Jodi Huelin
images by Entara Ltd.

Simon Spotlight
New York London Toronto Sydney

Hello, there. I'm Grandpa Piggley. Gather round and I'll tell you a story about when I was growing up down on Raloo Farm. *Jakers!* What fun we used to have . . .

Based on the TV series *Jakers! The Adventures of Piggley Winks* created by Entara Ltd.

Simon Spotlight
An imprint of Simon & Schuster Children's Publishing Division
1230 Avenue of the Americas, New York, New York 10020

Manufactured in the United States of America
First Edition
2 4 6 8 10 9 7 5 3 1
ISBN-13: 978-1-4169-0384-0   ISBN-10: 1-4169-0384-4

Piggley and his friends Ferny and Dannan were late for school. "Excuse me, coming through," said Hector, bumping into Millie and knocking her book to the ground.

"I'll get that," said Ferny.

"Thank you," said Millie.

Suddenly Ferny found himself staring at Millie. "Uh . . . I . . . you're welcome," he mumbled.

"Come on, Ferny!" Piggley called. "Hurry up!"

"We're late!" Dannan added. Piggley and Dannan wondered what had gotten into their friend—he was walking so slowly.

"Jakers!" Piggley exclaimed. "You must have scrambled your brain when you picked up that book!"

At school Ferny could not concentrate. He drew hearts all over his paper while daydreaming of Millie. Ferny couldn't stop thinking about her.

Ferny did some silly things to try to get Millie's attention. First he turned a few cartwheels in the classroom.

At recess Ferny walked right into the path of Hector on the swingset. *Shoosh!* Up Ferny went, swinging alongside Hector. And after the bell sounded, Ferny walked backward— right over a picnic bench!

"What's *wrong* with you, Ferny?" Piggley asked. "You've been acting like a sleepwalking sheep all week!"

"Nothing's wrong," Ferny replied. "I'm fine."

But Dannan knew what was going on— *Ferny has a crush,* she thought. "Ferny likes Millie," Dannan declared.

As the friends walked home from school, Ferny described his feelings. "I've tried everything to get her to notice me . . . but *nothing* works," he said. "Maybe I'll ask Millie to go swimming at the pond."

Dannan didn't like that idea. She thought Ferny should act heroic, like in the movies. "You could be Millie's knight!" Dannan suggested.

Ferny thought his idea was simpler, but he figured that Dannan must know what girls like. And so he followed her advice.

Back at Raloo Farm, Piggley and Dannan transformed their friend into a knight. Piggley gave Ferny a bucket to wear as a helmet. Dannan added a barrel lid for a shield and a scrap of cloth for a banner.

Ferny was still unsure about the plan. But he promised Dannan he would be brave and loyal and always ready to rescue a damsel in distress. Piggley and Dannan showed Ferny the final addition to his knightly role. "Here's your gallant steed," said Dannan.

"You mean Finnegan!" exclaimed Ferny. "Janey Mack, this might be fun after all!"

Ferny hopped aboard Finnegan, and Piggley and Dannan walked beside him. Suddenly they heard a girl's voice. "I am going to get you!" yelled the voice.

"Jakers!" said Piggley. "That's Millie! It sounds like she needs help."

Down alongside the stream, Millie was playing tag with her friends Katrina and Fergal. But Ferny didn't know they were playing tag. He thought that Fergal had stolen Millie's hair ribbon and would not give it back.

"Hold on Millie, I'll save you!" Ferny exclaimed, heading down the slope toward Millie. Then Ferny's bucket helmet slipped and fell forward, covering his face. "Whoa! Oh, no!" Ferny yelled. He tumbled down the hill and landed in a muddy puddle at Millie's feet. *Splash!* Ferny splattered her with mud.

"I don't think that went well," said Piggley.

A defeated Ferny headed back up the hill. "I . . . uhh . . . sorry," he called. "I'll just go now."

Ferny thought about how he hadn't wanted to be a heroic knight in the first place. He didn't want to save the day. All he wanted to do was ask Millie to go swimming.

When Ferny got home he told his dad everything that had happened. "What do *you* want to do?" Ferny's dad asked. Ferny explained that he wanted to invite Millie to go swimming at the pond on Saturday. "Sometimes you just have to trust yourself," his dad said.

*Should I follow my dad's advice?* Ferny wondered. He had followed Dannan's advice and, though she meant well, her plan had not quite worked out.

"Jakers!" said Ferny. "I will go talk to Millie!"

Later that day when Ferny saw Millie he mustered the courage and asked.

"Millie, would you like to go swimming
with us at Dannan's pond tomorrow?"
"Ferny, I'd love to!" Millie replied.
Ferny was thrilled. He had trusted
himself and everything worked out.